IN THE BACKGROUND
IS A WALLED CITY

BOOKS BY MICHAEL HEMMINGSON

FOR BORGO PRESS / WILDSIDE PRESS:

The Rose of Heaven
Barry N. Malzberg: Beyond Science Fiction
How to Have an Affair and Other Instructions
Judas Payne

FOR OTHER PRESSES:

The Naughty Yard (Permeable Press, 1994)
Crack Hotel (Permeable Press, 1995)
Minstrels (Permeable Press, 1997)
The Mammoth Book of Short Erotic Novels (Carroll & Graf, 2000)
The Mammoth Book of Legal Thrillers (Carroll & Graf, 2001)
Wild Turkey (Forge, 2001)
The Comfort of Women (Blue Moon, 2002)
The Dress (Blue Moon, 2002)
Seven Women and Other Stories (Bookspan, 2003)
My Fling with Betty Page (Eraserhead Press, 2003)
Drama (Blue Moon, 2003)
The Rooms (Blue Moon, 2003)
The Lawyer (Blue Moon, 2003)
House of Dreams Trilogy (Avalon, 2004)
The Garden of Love (Blue Moon, 2004)
Expelled from Eden: A William T. Vollmann Reader (Thunder's Mouth Press, 2004)
The Las Vegas Quartet (Avalon, 2006)
Short & Sweet (Blue Moon, 2006)
Understanding William T. Vollmann (Univ. of South Carolina Press, 2008)
Star Trek: TV Milestone (Wayne State Univ. Press, 2008)
The Yacht People (Neon Books, 2008)

IN THE BACKGROUND IS A WALLED CITY

or,

HOW SANTA CLAUS & I SAVED THE WORLD

An Historical Memoir

MICHAEL HEMMINGSON

The Borgo Press
An Imprint of Wildside Press

MMVIII

CONTENTS

PART THE FIRST

PART THE SECOND

PART THE THIRD

PART THE FOURTH

for Liv Kellgren

ABOUT THE AUTHOR

MICHAEL HEMMINGSON writes books in every possible genre he can: literary, western, SF, horror, noir, autobiography, erotica, narrative journalism, gonzo journalism, cultural anthropology, critical theory, critifiction, ethnography, and many other modes of academia including post-postmodern and post-colonial treatises. And private eye yarns. And film and TV studies. And smut. He also writes plays and screenplays. He has two independent feature films out: *The Watermelom* (LightSong Films) and *Stations* (Hemlene Entertainment). He has produced, directed, and written plays in San Diego and Los Angeles for the Fritz Theater and The Alien Stage Project. He lives in southern California, where the dead and the unborn visit him nightly as his two cats (Worf and Poe) observe with indifferent, feline curiosity.

IN THE BACKGROUND IS A WALLED CITY

IT WAS HALF-PAST SEPTEMBER
WHEN THE RED PHONE RANG.
—Harlan Ellison,
"Santa Claus vs. S.P.I.D.E.R."

FOR THE INFINITY OF ALL TIME AND SPACE,
ANYTHING IS POSSIBLE IF ONLY ONCE.
—Barry N. Malzberg,
Galaxies

PART THE FIRST

MY DAYS AS A GHOST-SEEING DWARF

EARLY YEARS, 3 ½ FEET TALL

Torn away from Heaven like a bright red and fresh turnip that was ripped from fertile soil just a little too soon: I was born. I was born five weeks premature in 1931 but I was going to make it. The doctors said I would probably be small most of my future days, but I would live. My father, however, did not. He got the call at work, at his office, that his dear young wife was in labor early; he rushed toward the hospital like a rampaging elephant and he was driving too fast, too erratic and there was a collision with several other cars and my father died on the scene—in fact, he was decapitated by the shattered windshield. He never saw me and I never knew him and "that was that," as they say. Here is the curious thing about my parents: it was one of those May/December deals, she was twenty-three and he was fifty-two. As far as I've been able to come up with, my father had a good friend in Tennessee, a man his age who had a teenage daughter and the daughter wound up eloping with her father's friend, causing her own father to disown her forever. It's a sordid little story and who knows if it was true; she was a lot younger than her husband but in Kentucky, 1931, no one paid much mind. When my mother found out about her husband's accident, she said, "Did he lose his mind? What am I going to do? I can't raise this child on my own," as I suckled her tragic bosom for the necessary milk.

Oh: I was also born with dwarfism but they (the doctors) couldn't really tell or didn't want to tell my mother.

She cried for many days, perhaps a whole week, and it was just too much for her: the post-labor blues and the loss of her spouse and security drove her to slit her wrists and jab the artery at her neck with a small pair of steel scissors.

Alas, I was an orphan but I didn't know any better, I was merely a week old. I was found crying and hungry near my mother's dead body, her blood all over the wood floor like a small lake. Her father—my grandfather—didn't want anything to do with me. "Toss him back out into the ocean," he told the authorities, "he's a runt, a bad catch, a useless fish, a bad egg." And so I was given

14

up for adoption; it didn't take long for me to be matched with the right family, a sterile couple who really wanted a baby—Mr. and Mrs. Irwin Stonecutter of Coldwater, Kentucky. He was twenty-eight and she was twenty-six; they had been high school sweethearts and were devout Catholics who quietly thought that their inability to procreate was a punishment handed down by God for some sin they forgot about, or sin they would commit in the future. *We are not bad people,* they prayed, *O Lord please give us a child!*

Be careful what you wish for, eh; for there I was: a devil spawn in the flesh, according to my grandfather. Even when he was dead and a ghost, he didn't have anything good to say to me.

Nevertheless, the Stonecutters didn't care that I would never grow to the size of a normal human being; they were just happy to have a child to hold and call their own.

I didn't start to see and speak to ghosts until I was five; maybe I could perceive them in the world before and I thought they were wispy people who fluttered about, who knows. The first ghost who came to me was my mother. She appeared in my bedroom one night. The room became cold with her presence but I was not afraid.

—*Look at you,* she said so softly, *you're growing up just fine. I'm so sorry I had to leave you, Jacob,* she said.

"My name is William," I told her.

—*That's the name your false parents gave you. The name I gave* you *is Jacob.*

This is when my father's ghost appeared. He was a tall and handsome man, better looking than my adopted father.

—*It's true, son,* said my ghost father, *your name is Jacob.*

"I like William," I said.

They both smiled.

—*We wish we were with you in this world,* they both said.

"Who are you?" I asked, even though I knew.

They told me and I didn't understand: how could they be my mother and father when I had a mother and father?

—*You have something important to do,* said my ghost mother. She bent down and kissed me on the forehead. I didn't feel the touch of her lips, but I could sense the love in her heart. The love made me feel warm.

Then they vanished.

In the morning, I told my mother about the visitation, and that the man and woman claimed to be my "real mother and father." Imagine her shock from hearing such a thing!

16

Michael Hemmingson

For one, I didn't know I was adopted yet; and two, such a visitation did not bode well inside the Catholic mind of my apparent mother, Mrs. Stonecutter.

"It was a dream," said she, "a very bad dream that you should forget about."

"I was awake," I said.

"You were asleep," she said.

"I was awake!" I said.

She slapped me across the face and said, "You were *a*sleep, do you under*stand* me, William Stonecutter?"

My face was red and I was crying.

"Do you *under*stand me, William *Stone*-cutter?"

"Yes, Mama."

"Good."

"I'm sorry, Mama."

"Go to your room and say ten 'Hail Mary's' and ten 'Our Father's. '"

"Yes, Mama."

THE GHOST FOLK

My ghost parents visited me that night. I said, "You are not real and I am only dreaming."

—*We are not flesh,* said my ghost mother, *and you are awake.*

—*You aren't dreaming, son,* said my ghost father.

I asked them why they left me and they wept in response and said how sorry they were. Then they smiled and sang me songs, songs they said came from Heaven. I didn't tell my adopted parents about this visit, or any of the others during the following years. I didn't tell them about the dead people I saw and sometimes talked to; I learned that certain things in life you keep quiet about or else they'd cause you trouble.

When I was seven, we moved from Coldwater, Kentucky to Niagara Falls, New York.

I was ten years old when I finally confronted my adopted parents and they broke down and confessed I was not their flesh and blood offspring. They wept, but they did not sing; and they did not say they were sorry. I told them I was all right with this because I had always known.

"How?" asked Mrs. Stonecutter.

"You *know* how," I said.

"What does he mean?" said Mr. Stonecutter to his wife. "What is he saying, dear?"

She said, "He dreams too much, I think."

My First Encounter
with Santa Claus

The Christmas Eve when I was eleven, I caught Santa Claus in the house. My dead grandfather, who rejected me when I was an infant and tormented me from time to time in my youth, came into the room and shouted for me to wake up.

—*I know you can hear me!* he cried.

I told him to go away.

—*Don't you sass me, you demon child!*

"Leave me alone."

—*Go to the living room now and look, you won't be disappointed.*

I knew if I didn't do what my dead grandfather wanted, he'd harangue me all night. So I went to the living room. It may have been 3:30 A.M. By the tree I saw a large man in a red suit with white trim and a red cap pulling presents out of an old burlap sac.

"Santa," said I, and there must have been the biggest smile on my face.

His back arched straight up and he turned around; the oatmeal raisin cookie I'd left out for him was half way in his mouth.

"Santa, it *is* you!" I said. I started toward him, to give him a hug, but he stepped back and almost fell over his bag.

"Arrragh," is the sound he made as the cookie fell out of his mouth and onto the floor.

I asked, "Santa, what's wrong?"

He looked at me suspiciously.

"Santa?"

"Who *are* you?" he said.

"Don't you know? I'm Wil—"

"Little Billy Stonecutter, I know. But how *the hell* can you see me, kid?" He thought about this. "Oh, yes, I remember now. You have a special gift, or curse some might say."

"You mean not everyone can see you?" I asked the jolly fat man who wasn't looking so happy at the moment.

"Well, I'm a spirit, after all—or half spirit you can say. Let's just say I don't actually reside in the dimension common folk normally see things. But you see four or five dimensions, do you not?"

"I don't know."

"Well, Billy, you're not *supposed* to see me."

"Why?"

"Be*cause* I'm not supposed to be real!" Now he laughed, and his belly did shake like a bowl full of jelly!

I was very excited.

"What did you bring me, Santa?"

"Oh, come now," he said, stepping toward me and kneeling. He put his hand on my shoulder and looked me in the eyes. His own eyes were very blue and twinkled like a clear night's sky full of stars. "Now, now," he said, "you know you're supposed to wait until morning."

"But it is morning," I said.

"Don't give me any smart talk, lad; you know what I mean. When the sun comes up and everyone is full of cheer."

"Can't you give me a hint, Santa?"

"Don't push it."

"Oh, okay."

"Go back to bed."

"If I must."

"You must. Now scoot and skedaddle."

My head hung low and I turned around and shuffled my feet like the dejected boy that I was.

"And oh, young Billy Stonecutter," said Santa.

22

I smiled and turned my head. "Yes?"

"No word of our little encounter to your parents, okay?"

"None at all?"

"No."

"But—"

"You listen to me."

"Okay."

"You give me your word, or else I'll never come visit you again, boy"

"My word," I said, very softly.

"We'll see each other again someday, William Stonecutter."

"We will?"

"I have a feeling."

"When?"

"You go back to bed now and sleep."

In my bedroom, my dead grandfather appeared and said:

—*He always was a bastard.*

"Go away!" I said, covering my face with a pillow.

Next, my dead mother appeared, alone. She sat on the bed and sang me a lullaby. I didn't think I'd be able to sleep, but I did.

THE WAR

When I was sixteen, I wanted to enlist in the Army to go overseas and fight the Nazis from taking over the world...or fight the Japanese from doing the same...either way, I wanted to serve my country because that's what a man did in those trying and scary times.

You can guess what happened.

I went down to the enlistment office and was laughed at.

"Join the circus!" the officers said.

"Join the circus!" the men standing in line for physicals said.

—Join the circus! said the ghosts of those dead soldiers who hung around the place and tried to whisper into the ears of the men who were going off to die:

—Hey, buddy, don't do it!

There was, in fact, a circus setting up on the outskirts of the city. I took a bus out there and met with a man called The Ringmaster. He was seven feet tall and had a thick brown mustache. He wore a red suit, but it was not like Santa's suit.

"Who are you?" he asked, looking down.

"My name is William," I said, looking up—way up.

My mother's ghost appeared behind the man.

—*Your name is Jacob!* she hissed at me.

"William Jacob."

"I am the Ringmaster." He stared down at me like I was an ant. He asked, "And what can I do for you, young master William Jacob?"

"Well, sir," I said, shuffling my feet, "I was hoping you may have work for me."

"Ha, ha."

"Ha?"

"Ha," he said.

I didn't understand.

"That's what I thought," he said.

"I need a job," I told him, "I need a purpose in this life."

"Don't we all. But, alas, as you can see for yourself, I am ankle deep in little people and I'm afraid to inform you, son, I don't need anymore," and he gestured, and I followed his arm and his pointing finger, and I saw in the distance (I had to squint, for my eyesight wasn't all that good) half a dozen human beings my size, waddling and working, whistling and wandering, putting up tents and hammering nails into pieces of wood.

"I can do more than labor," I said softly, my self-esteem lower than my height.

"They also dress up like little clowns and hop up and down and make the kids and adults laugh out loud," said the Ringmaster.

"Oh."

"Do you have any special talents, young Jacob, William?"

"Well," I told him, "I see and talk to ghosts."

"Drive that car by me again, son?"

"Ghosts," I said, "they talk to me, and I talk to them."

"Bahh!" he said. "Pfui!" he said. "Ho-hum," he said, "I have two women who can do that and who needs them? I ask again: who needs 'em? Who gives a hoot what the dead have to say? This world is for the living, boy. Tell me something I don't know."

—*Tell him his circus days are over,* said my mother.

I gave my mother a look.

"What're you staring at?" said the Ringmaster.

"I have a twitch."

"How unfortunate."

26

"I don't want to waste your time," I said, "do you have work for me or not?"

"I'm sorry."

"I'll take that as a no."

"These are trying times, short fellow."

I walked away.

The other dwarves yelled at me: "There's too many of us in the world!"

I waited for the bus back to the city. It was going to be a long wait; this particular bus only came around every two hours.

—*He will soon realize what a fool he is,* said my mother.

"Go away."

—*What?*

"I said go away."

—*I'm your mother!*

"Would you go away and leave me alone?!?" I cried.

She looked hurt, and vanished.

I once heard a soup line proverb: "Be careful what you ask for: you may or may not get it—and either way what you get is pure hell."

After that day, I would never see my mother, father, grandfather, or any other ghost.

* * * * * *

The Nazis bombed the city while I was on the bus. No one knew they had managed to move their bombers here without detection. Some would later say they had help from people in the government who'd sold their souls to Hitler. What did it matter how those Krauts got here, they were here, they invaded, they took over.

They dropped bombs on the circus tent, fulfilling my mother's prophecy.

They bombed the city I lived in.

They bombed Washington, D.C., killing the President and a lot of senators and people's representatives.

A bomb exploded near the bus I was on. The bus flipped over. The people around me were hurt, and some were killed.

* * * * * * *

I lived.

I woke up, in pain and bleeding. But I was alive.

I had a broken arm and three broken ribs, but I was alive.

I had blood in my hair and in my eyes, but I was alive.

I walked away from the horror.

There were dead people all around me, but I didn't see any of their ghosts.

28

MICHAEL HEMMINGSON

* * * * * *

I made my way into the city, which was
on fire from all the bombs. So many confused, crying, terrified people. Nazi troops
were beginning to march in. When the Nazis
pointed their guns at me, I held up my hands
and was taken prisoner; those who didn't
were immediately shot.

"The United States of America no longer
exists," I was told when I was processed into
a labor division. "You are now a citizen of
the Extended Fatherland."

* * * * * *

Something was wrong. I could no longer
see.

* * * * * *

"Mother, Father," I said, "where are you?"

* * * * * *

As far as I could figure, the injury to my
head caused me no longer to be able to see
and talk to the dead. I was just like everyone

29

else now. In one way, this was a relief; in another, I never felt so empty alone.

* * * * * * *

I was placed in a factory to work. We processed metals and steels taken from the fallen city to make more tanks and cannons and such.

"Do not view your height as a curse," one Nazi office told me, "but an asset. While America may have shunned you, Germany embraces you. You can go far, small man, far in this new world, if you set your heart and mind on doing so."

PART THE SECOND

IN SEARCH OF THE MISSING SANTA CLAUS

THE LETTER

Eventually, there became ways to get letters out to places where, through normal channels, such *communiqués* would not be possible. When I was twenty years old, I sent this letter to the North Pole:

Dear Santa,

Do you, perhaps, remember me? There was a night, ten years ago, when I saw you and we spoke to one another. I am hoping you remember me because I doubt few kids can actually see you, and at the time I had a certain gift. I am sure you remember me because I was pretty short, even for a kid.
Anyway, let me get right to the point: where the hell are you?

Where the hell are you when the world really needs you right now, you old bastard?

I mean really, look at the world, look at America; there hasn't been a Christmas for years, and I don't think it has anything to do with the Nazis and the Japs. I think it's because you don't come to homes and to children (and adults!) anymore.

Have you given up on us?

Have you forgotten us?

Please come back. We need you.

OK? OK.

Sincerely yours,

William "Jacob" Stonecutter

LOSS OF FAITH

For a year, I cursed the name, idea and memory of Santa Claus. He never replied to my letter, he never showed up the next Christmas, and life in America continued to be hell under German and Japanese occupation. Many times I thought of doing myself in, cashing my own check, punching my own time clock...I guess it's a good idea I didn't. My ghost mother was right: I had a mission in this life.

SOMETHING OVERHEARD

"Two years ago, I saw Santa Claus," a drunk said.

"Bullshit," I said.

I was also drunk. There were a bunch of us factory workers drunk, drinking, nowhere to go, hanging out in the alleys and the parks, away from the Nazi patrols, nothing to our lives in the off-hours but booze, dreams, and talk of days that I started to think never happened.

"What do you know," said the drunk, "what does a half-man like you know about anything, eh?"

"Get stuffed!" I laughed. "You didn't see anything, Mr. Five-Foot-Ten, Mr. Days Gone Bye."

"I did see him!" the drunk yelled at me. "He came to my house, he stood there and mumbled, 'What am I doing here? All is lost

36

forever.' And then he went back up the chimney. Didn't leave a damn present, the bastid."

"The what?"

"The bastid, that's what he is."

"Don't you talk about Santa like that!" I yelled, even though my sentiments were the same.

The drunk laughed. "And what are you gonna do? Kick my ass?"

I HAVE A PURPOSE

The next day, when I was sober and working at the factory, I knew what I had to do. I was, in fact, somewhat happy and feeling a tad bit hopeful that the world, indeed, may not be doomed to make its way to hell in a hand basket after all.

In other words, I had an idea.

A crazy idea, but it was a crazy world, so what the hell!

Eh? Ha, ha.

So that night, after work, I escaped the city.

Northbound

Getting out wasn't too hard, especially for a dwarf.

A regular-sized man could make his way out of the city limits if he set his heart on the matter; the Nazi border guards were lazy and even they knew there was nothing better in either direction—so what if someone left the city? There was no nirvana, there was no sanctuary, there was no Shangri-la to be found and have. What these German bastards didn't know was that there was a North Pole and in the North Pole lay all the hope mankind could ever have to offer...and that hope, I now knew, lay dormant in the ice like cicada in the distant ground.

Like I said, getting out wasn't hard...I walked through the empty fields away from the border guards, carrying a bag full of canned food, small bottles of water, two changes of underpants and three paperback novels:

Gulliver's Travels, by Jonathan Swift;
Around the World in Eighty Days, by Jules Verne;
The Big Sleep, by Philip Marlowe;

and let me tell you, brothers and sisters, in the weeks that lay ahead, these books became my friends: I read and re-read them many times, I knew the words inside and out, this way and that; and I came to understand that the stories of our times are the stories that keep us going.

A CHANCE ENCOUNTER WITH THE FORMER RINGMASTER WHO DIDN'T BELIEVE IN ME

"Hey, you," said a familiar voice, "yes, you…stop right there…brother, have you got a dime? Brother, can you spare some food? Brother, do you have a heart of hearts and can you spare some pity on a wretched soul who had it all and lost it all and now has lost all hope for life itself? That is, my friend, help me the hell out, eh? I say, 'eh'?"

The voice was coming from the dark shadows of barren land. It was just after midnight and there were plenty of stars in the sky. I stopped and my head tingled like it sometimes did when I used to talk to the dead. I *knew* that booming voice, *damn-it-all-to-hell*—I knew it from my past; I knew that voice from the day the Nazis bombed the city and I knocked my head on metal and lost my supposed gift. (I still wasn't sure if I was happy or sad about that.)

"Who be there, I ask?" I asked.

"No one," replied the baritone voice that had no body.

"Are you a spectre?"

"Alas, I am still flesh and blood," and he showed himself, he appeared so that the light from the half-moon crossed across his body like a beacon. He smelled, but all men smelled those days because baths were a rarity; his clothes were old and tattered and lost their red hue; he stood before me, all seven feet of him; he looked down upon me and said, "A, a dwarf! I knew many in my day. Alas, they are all dead now. Tell me, Master Little Man, why does your face look so familiar to me? Have you and I seen each other in this life before?"

"Indeed we have, sir. Are you not the Ringmaster?"

"Yes, they called me that once. Now they call me Oscar."

"Oscar?"

"The name my sweet little mum gave me oh-so-long-ago."

"I thought you were dead, when the Nazis bombed your circus tents."

"I was the only one who lived," and he sounded very cumbersome and lost when he

42

spoke those words. "I should have died with my friends. I think I would be happy dead… nay, I *know* I would. I'm too much of a coward to take my life, so I live out here, in the middle of nowhere; I live out here like a shadow and await any scrap of food that may come my way. Some say I am a cannibal and eat the flesh off those who pass, but this is not true. I am not a bad man. I am tall, I am hopeless, but I am not bad."

"No," I said, "you are not a bad man, sir."

"If I may say so, I was once a man in a high castle."

"Indeed you were, Oscar."

"And may I ask your name, small one?"

"You may call me William."

"How about Bill?"

"If you wish."

"So where do I know you from, Bill?"

I wanted to chastise him for not hiring me that day; but if he had, would I have died during the bomb raid? And did the past and all its sorrows and rejections matter anymore?

"I was once a fan," I told him.

"A fan!"

"I loved your circus."

"Well, how about them apples."

"Apples are good."

"Those were the days, eh?"

"They were indeed, Oscar."

"So, my fine little friend, I ask again: can you spare a dime?"

"I have no money," I said, "but I do have food."

"Oh, how I love food," he said with a smile.

"In fact," and I reached into my backpack, "I have an apple!" and I handed it to him.

"A fine green and ripe apple," and he bit into the fruit; "so juicy, so tasty, so hard… with the aroma of heaven."

"Oh, yes," I said, biting into my own apple—my last one, and it wasn't all that ripe or tasty but I figured we all had our perspective on things.

My food rations were quickly dwindling, too.

* * * * * * *

I also shared a can of pre-baked beans with Oscar. "They taste better cold than heated," I said, "at least I tell myself this."

"I haven't had a warm meal since…." He had to think about that. "Since the day the Nazis invaded. Yes. Probably. It doesn't matter. Food is food."

I muttered, "We are in hell."

He said, "It seems so, yes. But there are degrees of hell. Perhaps we are lucky to be in

German occupied land. I hear on the Japanese occupied West Coast—in California, Oregon and Arizona—things are worse, much worse. Public executions, the rape of white women, eighteen-hour work days, walls being built around the cities so no one can ever leave."

"I've heard the same."

"Maybe we are better off here," he said, "maybe this is truly the best of both possible worlds."

"I like the sound of that," I said as we finished off the cold beans.

"So what are you doing out here in the land of nowhere, Bill?" he asked, adding: "If I may be so bold as to ask."

"I am heading North."

"A jaunt?"

"A journey."

"A trek?"

"A mission."

He said, "There is nothing in Canada—they made their dirty deal with Hitler and his ilk. Damn them!"

"I am going beyond."

"To where?"

"My destiny," I said with pride, "is the North Pole."

"Oh? Why?"

So I told him: I told him everything.

He nodded and said, "I see."

"OK," I said, "so you think I'm mad."

"Not at all."

"Crazy."

"No."

"Loony."

"Perhaps, but these are insane times, eh? I say, 'eh'?"

"Eh," I replied, "I guess so."

There was a long pause as we sat there in the cold hours before sunrise.

"My friend," he said, "William," he said, "I would like to join you on your quest," he said.

"Drive that by me again," I said.

"I would like to tag along, and help."

"Do you even believe in Santa?"

"Of course I do...the question is: does he still believe in me?"

I didn't know.

"Well?"

I didn't know.

I said, "Yes."

"Is he even up there?" asked Oscar.

I said, "Where else would he be?"

"Will he help?"

"He has to," I said, "I know this."

Oscar nodded and said, "He has a duty."

"It's not like I have anything else better to do," I said.

"And I can say the same for myself."

46

There we were.

"Eh?" he said.

"Eh," I said.

He smiled.

"You really want to tag along?" I asked.

"I want to help. I want to have purpose again."

"We leave at first light, sir!"

"Hell, let's leave now," he said, stretching his elongated arms and legs, "better to move during darkness, eh."

"Yeah," I said, "who needs sleep, eh."

"Sleep is overrated."

"That's what I heard."

"Where?"

"Here and there."

"Let's go save the world, young master William," he said, "and all of your courage in such a few feet."

"Hey, brother," I told him, "let's get something straight from the get-go: you don't make fun of my lack of height, I don't give you grief for your abundance of such, okay? Eh? I say, 'eh'?"

Oscar bellowed like a trumpet; he reached down and lifted me up into the sky and planted me onto his shoulders like I was his child and he was a father about to take me for a walk around the proverbial block.

"I have food in me," he said, "and the food and our quest is my fuel…we can make better time if I use my long legs. No offense, OK, but your short legs can't move as fast as mine."

"Offense?" I was giddy with new hope. "Never!"

"Off we go then, Bill."

"Onward!"

ONWARD

I was afraid what would happen when we ran out of food, and it was obvious that Oscar needed much more than me to keep on going.

FORESHADOW

"Santa Claus *better* be there when *we* get there," said Oscar; "if he's not, some day I will find him and I will strangle his neck with these hands. *These* hands here, eh." They were very big hands.

"He is there," I said; "I feel it."

"I hope you are right," he said.

"I have to be right," I said.

DREAM

That night, I dreamt I was not correct in my assumption…and Oscar killed *me* with his exquisitely big hands.

MORNING

"Wake up," Oscar said, shaking me, "wake up, little man, and tell me why you are whimpering and uttering my name."

"Because I dreamt you died a horrible death at the hands of our enemies," I lied to him.

"How nice," he said with a grin, "now get up, we have progress to make."

So we continued North and found that getting across the border was very easy. There were no Nazi patrols anywhere.

OUR FIRST ALLY

In Canada, we met a robust man with green eyes and black knee-high boots; he had a long beard and long hair and was smoking a cigar. He was also pointing a double-barreled sawed-off shotgun at us.

"Well, looky here," he chuckled, "aren't you quite the pair: a half-pint and a giant."

"My dear sir," Oscar said, "we don't want any trouble."

To that I concurred: "None at all."

"But you've found it," said the robust man with green eyes; "you're trespassing on my property."

"We didn't know," said Oscar.

"Can't you read the signs?"

"We didn't see any signs."

"There are signs everywhere."

"That's always been my problem, I suppose."

"So what are you fellows? American or German? Because you sure aren't from around here."

"We're," I started.

He cocked the shotgun. "Or are you Nazi spies?"

"Why would we be spies?" asked Oscar.

"Spies everywhere."

"I can assure you, we are not."

"Yeah, well," and then the robust man with green eyes fired. "Oh shit," he said, and Oscar groaned and clutched his stomach. There was blood. Oscar fell to his knees. "Oh shit," said the robust man, "I didn't mean to shoot. This goddamn hair-trigger thing…"

"Ugh," went Oscar.

"You killed him!" I said.

"Nah, no pellets," said the man, "just rock salt."

"Oscar?" I said.

Oscar said, "Hurts like hell, that's for sure, but I'll live."

"Can you walk?" asked the man.

"I think so," said Oscar, standing up.

"Come," said the man, "we'll fix you right up."

* * * * * * *

We went to his house, which was basically a large empty cabin. He said his name was Gabriel Nash. "I only meant to scare you off," he said, "you never know these days. I truly am sorry for any pain I've caused you."

"There's plenty of pain," Oscar said; when he chuckled there was a horrible expression on his face: "Ouch. Well, at least I know I'm alive and it feels good to feel alive."

Gabriel asked Oscar to take his shirt off and lie on the floor. Oscar did what he was told. There were many healed scars on Oscar's torso to which Gabriel said, "You're no stranger to pain."

"I was treated like an animal when I was a child," said Oscar.

"Them bastards."

"And them some."

"This is going to hurt like hell."

"It already does."

Gabriel handed Oscar a bottle of whiskey. "Drink this."

"Thank you kindly."

With a pair of tweezers, Gabriel proceeded to remove the rock salt from Oscar's flesh. It was a long, arduous and unpleasant sight and task; most of the time I couldn't look.

When the deed was done, the two men opened a second bottle and by this time they were laughing.

"Come, little man!" said Gabriel. "Share this bottle with us."

"Maybe I shouldn't," I said.

"Why not?"

"We are on a mission," I said.

"A proverbial quest!" said Oscar, drinking away.

"I must remain sober and keep my goal in sight," I said.

"Oh, you take one break and get drunk, my fine short friend," Oscar said as he handed me the bottle.

"Might I ask of this mission?"

Oscar and I (with pride, I must note) told him.

Gabriel nodded, drank, and nodded. "A noble journey."

"We'd like to think so," Oscar said, full of himself and whiskey.

"May I join you?" Gabriel asked.

Oscar and I looked at each other.

Gabriel said, "Look at my life here. I have nothing here. I think I could help you; I would like to help you. I would like to…get the hell out of here."

"OK," I said.

"Welcome aboard," Oscar said.

"Good," Gabriel said. "Let's whip up some dinner and get going."

AND SO...

Now we were three.

HOW WE BECAME FOUR

"Ringmaster! Ringmaster, is that you?!"

It was a woman's voice, high-pitched and sweet, coming out from the trees above us in….

We'd been walking for almost a week now; we were getting closer and it was getting colder. Snow was at our feet and in the branches from all these trees.

She emerged from the trees like an angel of doom, falling from the sky, gracefully landing on her feet. Her hair was matted down and dirty, her eyes large and crazy; she was barefoot and her body was covered in bloody animal furs.

"Why, it *is* you," she said, looking upon Oscar.

"Nadia."

"None other."

"Nadia?"

"It is I."

The two embraced.

"I thought you were dead!" said Oscar.

"I thought the same about you, Ringmaster."

"Obviously you were both wrong," Gabriel said, clearing his throat. "Mind introducing us to the lass?"

The woman eyed both Gabriel and myself. "Yeah, RingM, don't be so damn rude."

"These are my companions, Bill and Gabe. Companions, allow me to introduce Nadia the Nimble Nymph: the finest trapeze artist to ever grace any circus in this world."

She said, "Ain't so nimble after all these years, I'm afraid."

"Looks like you still got the moves the way you came out of the branches," Gabriel said.

"Is that a real compliment," she asked, "or are you just trying to be sweet on me, old man?"

"You still got what it takes, sister," Oscar said.

"Here I am with two and a half men; how could a girl be so lucky? I'm surprised I still know how to speak English. I hardly talk to anyone. I don't know when's the last time that I did. Is that sad or is that bad?"

"It is what it is, sister."

"So wait. What the hell are you doing up here out in the middle of nowhere?"

"We are heading to the North Pole," I said.

"Oh? Well; it's not that far away, let me tell you. And you seem to be going in the right direction. Just follow your nose, or your instincts, or the Northern Star. The Big Question is: why?"

We told her.

"Well, I'll be," she said. "Holy smoke," she said. "Can I come along?" she asked. "Can I help?"

"It will get mighty cold," said Oscar.

"I know cold. I have more furs. I even have furs you boys can use."

"You are an angel!" cried Gabriel.

"Yeah, yeah," she said, "let's go find Santa, why don't we."

AND SO... (2)

Along the way, we picked up half a dozen other allies, making the group ten. Who they are doesn't matter in this story, because history has talked about them in other books and even a movie or two. What the history texts that they teach in school nowadays leaves out is the ugly truth about Santa Claus.

But that's why I'm writing this memoir.

PART THE THIRD

THE NORTH POLE

Santa's Castle

In the foreground was a walled city and the wall was made of towering ice; beyond the wall was a crystal castle so high it seemed to be reaching for Heaven like the Tower of Babel. It glowed in the sunlight of the icy cold North Pole. It was a good thing we had all these furs Nadia had given us, as well as the pelts of a number of animals she happened to catch, kill, skin and cook up for the rest of our team to devour.

"This is it," I said, "we are here."

"At last," Oscar said.

"Finally," Gabriel said.

"Hot damn!" Nadia said.

The rest of the group (*i.e.*, the other six) agreed, and we were all pleased: the end of this cold, tiring trek had come to an end, and now a new set of problems was before us.

"Do you think he's still there?" asked Nadia.

"Where else would he be," said Oscar.

"Where else would a man like him go," said Gabriel.

"So what do we do now?" said Nadia; "do we just waltz on in there and say 'Hiya, we wanna talk to Jolly Ol' Saint Nick'?"

"Hmm," went Oscar, "I wonder if the castle is guarded?"

"Can't tell from here," said Gabriel, looking.

"I can go in there and do recon," Nadia suggested. "Assess the situation and come back with a report."

"Good idea," Oscar said, reaching down and kissing her on the forehead.

"No," I said; "no, I will go."

They all looked at me.

"I am small and can move about, undetected, easier."

They all nodded.

"He has a point," Gabriel said.

"Are you saying I can't do the damn job?" Nadia asked, and she looked insulted, hands on her hips.

"This was his calling," Oscar said, "his mission."

"OK," Nadia said.

"I will go into the city of Santa Claus, " I told everyone, "and within twelve hours, I shall return and report; if I don't, feel free to make your way in because if I don't return, something is wrong."

INTO THE CITY OF TOYS

I discovered no resistance; no guards, no centuries, no man or woman who said, "William, you cannot pass."

It was very, very cold; and I was hungry and feeling delirious. After all this time, all this dreaming, all these months walking with the people I had gathered, here I was: but what if Santa was not in his home? What if my quest, and my intuition, were wrong? What if this was all for nothing?

But my feet moved, and I made my way closer to the castle.

MICHAEL HEMMINGSON

"GO AWAY," SAID THE ELF

"Go away," he said again, "there is nothing for you here, small human."

"Small?" I said; "who you calling *small*, asshole? We're the same *height*, jackass. You should *talk*, jerk."

I found him walking the deserted streets of the city; he wore a grimy, fouled green and red outfit with a cute little hat and pointed-toe shoes, the image we've all been bombarded with when it comes to Santa's elves.

He was the only elf I encountered in the city, though; all the huts and houses seemed to be abandoned, and yet I could tell this place had once teemed with life, love and toy-making.

"What happened here?" I asked.

"Don't ask stupid questions," said the elf; he had a white beard and red eyes and smelled like home-fermented mead.

The elf sat down on a brick and said, "What are you doing here?"

"I'm looking for Santa."

The elf laughed.

"It's not funny," I said.

"No," he said, "it's not."

"Is he here?" I asked.

The elf shrugged and said, "The answer to that question could have many responses."

"Stop being difficult."

"It's in my nature to be a conundrum."

"Maybe you think you're funny," I said, "but look at me, brother: I am not laughing."

"Oh my," he said, "so what do you want?"

"I want to find Santa."

"Why?"

"To talk to him."

"Why?"

"I think he can help."

"Why?"

"Because I still have faith."

"Why?"

"Why not," I said. "Have you forgotten faith?"

"Yes," said the elf.

"That's too bad."

The elf shrugged.

"Do you still make toys?" I asked.

The elf laughed.

I looked away.

"Don't feel bad, friend," he said.

"I want to feel bad," I said, "it keeps me going."

A pause.

"Why are you here?" he said.

"To save the world," I said.

He laughed.

"You think I am a fool," I said.

"You are lost," he said, *"very lost."*

"No."

"There is no saving...."

"No," I said.

"I see inside your soul," he said, "I see that you are serious."

"Yes," I said.

"Yes," he said.

We stood there for a long time and just looked at each other.

"I don't understand," said the elf.

"You don't have to."

"What do you want?"

"All I need to do, at this point, is to talk to the old bastard."

"Hmm. Well, you can talk, but who knows if he'll listen."

"I'll take my chances."

"No one's stopping you."

"So why are you here?"

"You think an elf has anything else better to do?" he said. "Except for the filthy, insane debauchery you'll find up there in Santa's Castle?"

"What do I know," I said.

"You don't know crap."

"You're telling me, brother."

"See you later."

"I hope not."

"Be careful what you wish for."

"Yeah?"

"Yeah."

"Why?"

He laughed at me and walked away.

FINDING SANTA

What I stumbled upon, I was not prepared for. To say that I was stunned and appalled would certainly be an understatement. My jaw dropped and I would have wept if I hadn't gotten so angry.

Santa was in one of the toy-making rooms, but he wasn't making any toys. The fat man was buck-naked and doing unspeakable sex acts with three undressed, very pink female elves.

I can't even bring myself to describe what Santa was doing, so I will let you, the Reader, use your dirty imagination (if you have one). Or you could choose not to believe me, that I am writing blasphemy, that nothing in my account is true.

"SANTA!" I screamed. "SANTA HOW COULD YOU?!?"

Santa looked up. He was holding a bottle of Finnish vodka in his left hand. The female elves squealed, appeared embarrassed, scrambled for their elfin attire, and quickly left the toy room.

"Who the fuck are you," he said, "and how dare you interfere with my fun time?"

"Oh, Santa, how could you."

"How could I indeed. Who are you to judge me? What the fuck are you? You're not an elf."

"You don't recognize me, Santa?"

"No. Should I?"

"I thought you knew us all."

"I'd need my glasses. Where are they? Oh, there. Okay," he said, putting on his spectacles and squinting, "well, yes, yes, I do remember you. Billy, is it? William. We met once."

"Yes."

"You saw me."

"Yes."

"When I was part spirit and part man."

"You remember."

"How could I forget? Few can see ghosts."

"I lost that gift. But I see you now."

"Because I have decided to be nothing more than a man," he told me. "I've said to hell with my inner ghost."

"Oh, Santa," I said, shaking, "this is horrible."

74

"The world is horrible, little guy! You know this, you have seem for yourself!"

"I don't understand…."

"*Fuck* understanding. *What* are you doing up here in the North Pole anyway? *What* are you doing in my castle? *What* are you doing getting your little nose into my playtime? I was getting my *rocks* off, boy. Those little elf bitches do things that—"

"*Stop! Stop! Stop!*" I cried, my hands to my ears and my eyes to the ground.

"My are you a prude."

"Santa doesn't *do* those things."

He chuckled: *ho, ho, ho.* "My you are naïve."

I sat down on a wooden chair and cried.

"Don't be sad, William. There's too much sadness in this fucked up world as it is."

I could not stop crying.

"You think you know who Santa is," he said, "but the sad fact is: you don't know doodly-squat!"

SANTA'S STORY

"Most do not know my true tale," he said, "they prefer their preconceived notions and the fairy tales and the gossip. *To those who believe otherwise, I say poppycock and pfui!*" His cheeks got rosy, a glint formed in his left eye, his belly shook like a bowl of (yes!) jelly and his testicles dangled to and fro as he chortled like the grand being he was destined to be, and was. "What do you think of them apples?" he asked.

I, for the life of my three and a half feet, asked if he would please (please!) get dressed, I couldn't deal with his naked body any more. He said of course, found his red thermals, and slipped them on. He picked up a bottle of well-fermented cider and shared it with me as he spoke:

"In the beginning, I was but a man and Santa was only a dusty crimson dream. These were the days I lived on Mars. You've heard of Mars, haven't you? Of course you have. A fine planet, a bit cold and very red—where do you think the red in my suit comes from? The white is for the polar caps of Mars, where I was born, raised, and lived pan-dimensionally as both a man and a spirit. That's how we Martians were; why be one thing when you can be both? Ah, those were the days. Until the evil gas tyrants of Jupiter invaded. Oh, they were vile things, I tell you! A hundred feet long, gray, and they smelled something awful. They came in their gas ships and attacked Mars, took Mars over, and enslaved the survivors. You see the connection here, don't you? Like what the Nazis and Japs did to your country, the Jovian Gas Giants did to my home planet. Many of us managed to flee Mars. I came here with all my elves. They're Martians, too. I bet you didn't know that. Well, now you know. So we came here and were saddened to see that you only lived in the flesh dimension, that the spirit was beyond you, that you were not yet evolved. This was exactly one thousand, one hundred and eleven years ago, which tells me there must be something significant about this year, and your being here, because numerically that's 1111. When you have four ones in a row like that (and sometimes three) it denotes something profound. But I see by the look on your face you have no idea what I'm talking about. Very well. So where was I? Oh yes. We fled Mars and came here to Earth, living on the northern polar ice cap so we wouldn't interfere with the natural growth of you three-dimensionally-trapped human beings. But darn it all to tears it was depressing to look upon you folks, with your lack of hope, joy and splendor. You had no concept of the idea of giving. Or joy. Even the smallest of gifts will put a smile on the face and save a life. And so I had a great idea. I would give everyone gifts once a year. And where better to start than the children? Every child needs a toy or three. And you know the story from here. Every year, I went into the fourth dimension and me and my elves and flying reindeer (also natives of Mars) did our thing. For hundreds of years we did this, even through all your various wars and famines and disasters. And then Nazi Germany pops up like a demon from a glass bottle. Worse than Napoléon, worse than Genghis Kahn, worse than Torquemada, and they were all very bad eggs. Here comes Hitler and all his atrocities and his world domination, he gets Japan to join up, they take over the world and the world goes to poop. Oh, the horror, the horror, the terror, the tragedy! I couldn't take it anymore. Hitler broke my heart. He wasn't a bad child; he really was not, so I have no idea what went wrong. He was a good kid who liked to draw. He even left me a drawing of his one night when I visited the home he lived in with his sweet, kind mother. What went wrong? Did I never bring him the right and proper gift? Needless to say, I lost all hope for humanity, I gave up, I decided drinking and fucking was a much better thing to do. You should join me. You're a good egg. Stay here in the North Pole, stay in my city of ice. The Nazis and Japs will never make their way here; they wouldn't dare. You can live out your days in peace, William."

"That's not why I'm here, Santa," I said.

"Oh?"

"No."

"So why are you here?"

"To ask you to help."

"Help with what?"

"Help make the world a good place again."

He laughed very loudly and shook his head.

MY PLEA

"Please," I said, "hear me out."

He passed me the bottle of cider. I took a drink and gave it back to him.

He said, "Like the elephants go, I'm all ears."

So I told him—about my vision, my journey, the team of misfit hopefuls I picked up along the way, and my arrival. I told him that only he, Santa Claus, could help.

"Did you ever think of the pressure this would put me under?" he asked. "Did you ever think about my feelings? My heart? My lack of faith in humankind?"

"Well," I said, "no."

"Of course not. No one ever thinks that *Santa* has a heart."

"It's because of your heart that I traveled all this way. It's because of your love for us I am here."

"The only love I have these days is in my crotch. I hate to be to vile, but it's a dirty world I live on now, I might as well join the party."

"But what about Mrs. Claus?"

"What about her?"

"She's your wife!"

"You don't know," he said; "she was killed."

"What?"

"Dead."

"Oh, Santa…."

"She went to visit a friend in Norway. The Nazis came. They captured her, raped her, and murdered her."

"I'm so sorry."

He began to weep. "I miss her so."

THE EAVESDROPPER STEPS IN

During my whole conversation with Santa, someone was hiding in the shadows and listening. He began to cry too, when the subject of Mrs. Claus was brought up.

Santa wiped his eyes and seemed mad. "Who's there?"

Silence.

"Show yourself, busybody!"

I was tense.

The eavesdropper stepped toward us on four hooved feet. He was a reindeer with a glowing red rose.

"What are you doing, Randy?" asked Santa.

"I couldn't help myself, Santa."

"Oh come here, kid."

The reindeer went to Santa. Santa hugged him. Then Santa held the cider bottle to Randy's mouth and the famous reindeer took a very big and long swig.

"Ah, that hits the spot," said Randy.

"You shouldn't spy," said Santa.

"I'm sorry, but this dwarf is right."

"Oh?"

"You have to help."

"I don't *have* to do anything."

"But you're Santa. It's your job."

"My job is to bring joy in people's life, once a year and once a year only."

"But you haven't," I said, "not for many years."

"And I told you why."

"That is *why* you have to help," said Randy the Red-Nosed Reindeer. "You can bring joy again."

"*What* can I do?" asked Santa Claus. "What the *fuck* can I possibly do?"

"I have an idea," said Randy, and his suggestion was so shocking that the jaws of both Santa and I nearly hung to the ground in sheer and utter shock.

"That's insane, you red-nosed maniac!" Santa said, and finished off the bottle.

"The world is nuts," Randy said, "so why not go with the flow, you old Martian? Why not avenge your wife's rape and murder?"

SANTA MAKES UP HIS MIND

Drunk, with plenty of bottles of cider and mead, Santa, Randy and I trekked beyond the walls of the city and found my friends; who were pacing about and acting nervous.

"William!" Nadia cried, lifting me in her arms, hugging and kissing me. (We'd grown to be close in our journey.)

But my compatriots were less interested in my return and more aghast by whom I brought with me.

"Everyone," I said, "allow me to intro-duce to you to the one and only—that man of our childhood smiles—the very great and grand Santa Claus!"

"And I have gifts to keep your blood and bones warm and full of joy," said Santa, pass-ing around the bottles of spirits.

"Hooray for Santa!" everyone sang.

"I'm very flattered that you every one of you came here, just for me, even though I find your quest a tad batty."

Everyone was quiet and somber.

"The world *is* ugly an ugly motherfucker," said jolly St. Nick, "but it doesn't have to remain so. I should have done something long ago. I was in grief, I was in pain, I suffered a terrible loss, just as you all have. As humanity has. It took the courage and the beautiful heart of this little fellow here to open my eyes," and he laid a large hand on the top of my head. He smiled and added, "Thanks to Randy, who always shows his true colors in a time of need, I have a plan."

PART THE FOURTH

AND NOW FOR THE REST OF THE STORY

THE DOS AND DON'TS OF BEDTIME TALES FOR CHILDREN

"And?" said my eight-year-old daughter, Nicole, bouncy and agitated. "What was Santa's plan?"

"Yeah," said my seven-year-old son, William, Jr., just as anticipatory as his older sister, "what did Santa do?"

They were tucked into their beds on that cold winter night, three days before Christmas.

"That will have to wait, for tomorrow night's conclusion of your father's adventures in the days of the occupation," I said with a smile.

They both moaned.

"I hate cliffhangers!" cried Nicole.

"You always do this during bedtime tales," said William, Jr.

"It's not fair," said Nicole.

"It's not," agreed my son.

"You'll enjoy the story more, if you have to wait and wonder," I said. "Now, it's time for you to both sleep."

They moaned again.

"Enough of that."

The sighed.

"Goodnight, Daddy," they said.

"Goodnight, my sweets," I said.

I went to the master bedroom and joined my wife. She was reading a book of Nathaniel Hawthorne short stories. I cuddled next to her. She took off her glasses and said, "Maybe it's time for them to know the truth."

"Nadia," I said, "we've discussed this before."

"Yes, and they're older now, and the time for soft happy stories will do them no good. You and I were there," she said, kissing me on the forehead, "we were on the frontlines of the rebellion, we lost a lot of friends, and we owe our freedom to what Santa Claus did, no matter how horrible it was."

"I miss our old friends," I said. The war had ended fifteen years ago, America rebuilt itself, Nadia and I had married and started a family, but it all seemed like yesterday.

And in case you are wondering, my kids came out normal; they weren't dwarves.

"Life goes on," Nadia said.

"It does, doesn't it?"

I loved my wife so.

"'Ho, ho, ho,' as Santa used to say."

"Ho, ho."

THE TRUTH IS TOLD

Nadia and I sat our children down the next night.

"What the history books teach you in school is wrong," I started. "The stories they tell on TV, the cartoons and fairy tales, are sugar-coated to not reveal the ugly truth of the war."

"It's time you know the truth, because eventually you will," Nadia added. "Your father and I were there, no one knows the truth better than we do."

"No war, ever," I said, "is won without bloodshed and a little bit of evil."

"Oh come on," said my son, "get on with it!"

"What was Santa's Plan?" said my daughter. "Tell us about his Message of Peace and Love."

Nadia and I looked at each other.

"The watered-down story you hear is that Santa went to visit Hitler in the middle of the night, and like Ebenezer Scrooge, Hitler saw the light, he realized his wicked ways, denounced his reign of terror and took his own life as a sacrifice for the better of mankind. But that's simply not true. Hitler cursed at Santa and was about to call for his guards to come in and kill Santa. So Santa had no other choice but to murder Adolf Hitler, because it was the only thing he *could* do."

My kids gasped.

They didn't believe me.

"Santa would never *do* that," Nicole said.

"He would," my wife said, "and he did. There was no other way. I'm sorry, but it's time to grow up and smell the coffee."

"What?"

"You're silly, Mom."

"It was kill or be killed," I said, "and that's the way of war. But Santa didn't stop there. He next went to Tokyo and assassinated the Emperor of Japan. Next he went after key generals and territorial governors in the German and Japanese empires. The destruction of this leadership caused a breakdown in order and morale; it allowed the rebellion to move forward and defeat the occupying forces in America. Russian joined the effort, and Russia dropped their A-bombs on

Berlin and Hiroshima. The rest of what the history books write are pretty much true. But no one wants to make Santa look like a homicidal maniac; it works better if he's a hero."

"I guess he had no other choice," said my son.

"None of us did," said Nadia. "Your father and I have told you how we went up to the North Pole with a group of friends? Well, in the resistance fighting, many of them died. Only one other, except your father and I, survived."

"Uncle Oscar," said my son.

"Yes," I said.

"Where is Uncle Oscar these days?" asked my daughter.

"Oh," said my wife, "he still wanders around."

GROWING UP

"I'm wondering if we made a mistake, telling them the truth about Santa," I said to Nadia that night before we made love and went to bed. (If you are wondering how a dwarf and a six-foot-tall woman have sex, don't—some private things must remain a mystery.)

"It was time," she said; "they have to grow up sooner or later."

"They're still children."

"Kids grow up faster these days, in these times."

I couldn't argue.

"I wish it had been different," I said.

"It was Randy's idea in the first place, that red-nosed terrorist."

"No, I mean…I wish all our friends were still here. Especially Gabriel. I do miss him."

"I miss them all," she said, kissing me on the forehead, "I think of them every day."

GABRIEL'S DEATH

I dreamt of them almost every night, and I dreamt of war, and I dreamt of death. These were the things that caused me to not sleep well. Nadia had some pills the doctor gave her, that allowed her to get a full night's sleep despite what she dreamt of. I didn't like the pills, they made me drowsy, they made me more depressed in the morning than I was during sleep. Often I dreamt of the gun battle that happened in New Jersey, when we were fighting off some Nazis, and Gabriel stepped on a landmine and was blown into half a dozen pieces—it was gory, gooey and gross. I was an amateur solider and had never seen something like that happen to a man, let alone a friend of mine. I knew I would be haunted by that image for the rest of my life...and I was.

ANOTHER HAUNTING DREAM IMAGE

"Slaughter them all, Santa," a drunk Randy said, "make the evil-doers bleed...."

GRATEFUL

...And despite all my regrets of the past, I had much to be grateful for: there were no wars in the world (for now), I had a family, I had an office job, I was making good money, and I had a home. So why wasn't I living in bliss?

SEEING THE GHOSTS AGAIN

I did miss that gift I once had. I missed the ghosts. I'd been living with that "empty" feeling far too long. As fate would have it, the gift of sight *did* return just as abruptly as it had left. This happened on the day before Christmas. I was shoveling the snow out of the driveway and as I walked back toward the house (a nice suburban number in Halicong, PA, three blocks from where I worked as an insurance claims adjuster), I slipped on some ice and cracked my head on the pavement. It was a doosey and it hurt and I was bleeding and I passed out.

When I came to, Gabriel was standing over me.

—*You okay?* he asked.

"Yeah," I said, "is this a dream? What are you doing here?"

—*I've always been here, we just couldn't talk.*

Then I saw my mother.

—*Oh, William, you have to be more careful,* she said.

Then I saw my father.

—*That's quite a bump you got on the back of your noggin,* he said, and chuckled.

—*I'll say,* agreed Gabriel.

I sat up and said, "I don't get it."

Then all sorts of dead friends from the resistance showed up and greeted me.

I rubbed the area where my head hit the ground.

"Now I get it," I said.

—*I'm glad you can see me again,* said my mother.

I was too. Now I would be less alone in my life.

A SECRET

I decided I wouldn't tell Nadia about this change. She never believed my stories about conversing with the dead. If I told her I could once again, she would probably call in the men in the white jackets.

CHRISTMAS EVE

Like he did every year, Oscar showed up in a flashy suit bearing gifts and cheer. The kids were always happy to see their Uncle Oscar. They jumped up and down and he lifted them high into the air. He and Nadia gave each other a warm, nostalgic hug and then we all sat down and had a Christmas dinner, family-style. This time, though, the ghosts were all around us, and the ghosts were smiling and nodding with approval.

O<small>SCAR</small>

"Stay this time," I said to him as we stood on the porch and drank cognac, "I insist."

"I wish I could, old friend," said Oscar, "but you know I can't. I love to visit, but this is not my home."

"The guest room is always yours."

"The bed is always too small."

"I can have one specially made."

He smiled. "I must do what I was meant to do: wander. I have places to go…"

"Where?"

"…people to see…."

"Who?"

"Oh, Bill," he said, "the life you and Nadia have made is a good one. I'm proud of you both, hear, hear!"

I told him about the return of my gift.

"Are they around?" he asked.

"Gabriel is," I said, "so are some others."

IN THE BACKGROUND IS A WALLED CITY

"I live with the memory of the dead every day; I don't need to see them."

—*Tell the tall bastard I miss him,* said Gabriel, and I did.

"I miss him too," Oscar said, "and now, I fear, I must go."

"Come by more than once a year," I said.

"Perhaps I will. As for now, onward!" and The Ringmaster was gone.

SANTA'S IN TOWN

Neither Nadia nor myself had seen Santa since the resistance days, fifteen years ago. This was because he had returned to the pan-dimensional realms of the spirit, especially on Christmas Eve when he had to stop time and take on the task of giving gifts to the world. My children never questioned Santa's exis-tence—few did, although there was a popular opinion that Santa was created by the gov-ernment "because the people once needed a war hero, like Captain America or Batman." But Nadia and I had taught our children oth-erwise, and Nicole and William, Jr. knew we could not afford the elaborate presents that Santa always left.

But now I had my gift back, and I waited up all night for my old friend's visit. I was about to nod off (my head still in pain from the fall) when I heard the bells of the rein-deer, when I saw Randy's red glowing nose in the sky, when I heard Santa whisk in with the gentleness of wind chimes.

"I smell the slight aroma of warm pear cider on your breath, old man," I said in a whisper.

He turned around, startled, like he had that night when I was just a child.

"Why, William," said he, "you can see me again."

"Indeed, old man."

We embraced like brothers, like the former soldiers we once were—and the secrets of our violent life were now the threads of our shame.

He asked, "How?"

And I told him.

He nodded.

I could tell he wasn't happy that I could see ghosts again.

"I must go now," he said.

"No," I said, "stay a while. There's so much to talk about."

"There isn't anything to talk about," he said, "but the past. And the past weighs us down, my little friend. We must think of the future; but even that can hurt us. We must think of the present."

"The present is forever to you."

"I have many houses to visit."

"You have all the time in the world."

"I still grow weary."

"Let me come along," I said.

"Not possible, William."

"You don't want me to. Why?"

"It's best that you keep to your life and I keep to mine. I left a little something extra for your kids."

"At least let me say hello to Randy."

He nodded.

The red-nosed reindeer was drunk and had gained ten pounds since I last saw him. It wasn't necessary for him to be sober to guide the sleigh through fog and snow, as long as his nose glowed he did his job. The famous reindeer was very happy to see me and the feeling was mutual. We shared a bottle of cider and then Santa said, "We must go now."

"Work, work, work," said Randy.

"When will I see you again?" I asked.

"Next year, of course," Santa said, and ho-ho-hoed and yelled, "ONWARD!" to his reindeer and off they went, not making a single sound, not stirring a bug or a mouse or a human.

THE YEARS GO BY

Life goes on, as they say.

Each Christmas, Santa and I chatted for a while, I had a drink with him and Randy, and off they went. Every time our visits became shorter and less personal. My children grew up, went college, married and had their own children. Nadia and I were grandparents. I was retired. Our days were quiet and uneventful and the world did what the world did: more wars, more tyrants rose up to power and disappeared. Oscar stopped coming around.

Nadia passed away when I was sixty. Bone marrow cancer. There was nothing I could do. People worried that I was all alone, especially my children, but what they didn't know was that things hadn't changed all that much. Nadia was no longer in pain but she was still by my side, her ghost was always with me and we talked and talked like we had never talked before.

—Why didn't you ever tell me your gift had come back? she asked.

I shrugged.

—Oh you, she said and she hugged me and it was nice.

STORIES

"Grandpa, did you *really* know Santa?" asked one of my grandchildren as I sat her on my knee.

"Oh yes," said I, "we are old and dear friends."

"Then why did he disappear again? He went away once, then came back, and he went away again."

"Don't believe all the rumors and funny stories you hear, my sweets. Santa is still with us, he comes every year."

"But the stories people tell are different."

"What people?"

"Kids at school. Teachers too."

"What stories?"

"That it's really Santa's helpers and the elves who deliver toys, not Santa himself. Is he dead?"

I sighed the way grandfathers have shied throughout time. "No, he's not. He can never die."

"Is he hiding?"

I hesitated, and said, "No. He is with us."

"Will I ever get to see him?"

"Maybe one day," I said and smiled, "if you're good."

"I *am* good!"

"Yes you are," and I hugged my grand-child, "yes you are, my sweets...."

RICHARD M. NIXON

The late 1950s and early 1960s were an odd and curious time. I was an old man, a widower, and somewhat of a cynic. I was not interested in politics, but once again politics seemed to be interested in me.

One summer afternoon, Santa and Randy came to visit. They had two bottles of pear cider. I had been napping. I was napping a lot in my autumnal years and I liked it.

"Hey, old friend," said Santa.

"Good to see you again!" said Randy.

I said, "What's this? What's this? It's nowhere near Christmas."

"Why does it have to be Christmas," asked Santa, "to come see a friend?"

Randy: "Indeed."

Me: "And what do we have here?"

Santa: "Drink!"

Randy: "Would we come all this way empty-handed?"

And so they sat down with me and we shared the bottles.

And then they told me the real reason for their visit.

"There is a dangerous man in power right now," Santa said, "and he'll gain more power soon. I saw this in a vision, and this vision was not good."

"I saw it in a dream," Randy said, "and the dream was not good."

"The man's name is Richard M. Nixon," Santa told me.

"The Vice President?" I asked, confused.

"Yes."

"And why is he dangerous?"

"He will run against John F. Kennedy for the seat of the President. He will win. The conflict in Vietnam, that is beginning as we speak, will escalate to the point that the U.S. will go to war with Russia; that war with Russia will result in a nuclear conflict that will spread across Europe and even into China."

"Causing the destruction of three-fourths of the world," Randy added with his usual doom and gloom voice, his red nose dimming to an almost blackout.

"Why," I moaned, "why all the wars and death?! Doesn't mankind ever learn?"

Nadia's ghost was there.

She said: —*No, man never learns.*

"There is no learning in war," Randy said, "so man forgets the bad, and repeats it again and again."

We sat there for a while, the three of us, and then I asked: "So why have you come to me with this?"

"What we did to Adolf Hitler," Santa said, "we must do to Richard M. Nixon."

"Call it a 'pre-emptive strike,'" said Randy.

"No," I said, "no."

"Why not?" asked Santa.

"After Hitler, I made myself a promise, that I would never be involved with another death."

"But Hitler was necessary."

"Yes, it was. But I didn't like it."

"You never took any credit," said Randy, "you could have been a hero."

"I never wanted to be a hero," I said.

They both laughed.

"No one remembers a hero," I said.

Again they laughed.

—*They are right*, said my wife's ghost, *Nixon will destroy the world if he becomes President.*

"Hush," I said, closing my eyes.

"We will do it without you," Santa said.

"Then do it."

"We just wanted to be a team again," Randy said.

"I'm so old now…but you two never age."

They nodded, and we didn't speak of the matter anymore. We finished off the bottles, they left, and I went back to sleep.

THE ASSASSINATION

Three days later, it was all over the news on my small black-and-white TV, and in the papers, and the talk on the street—Vice President Nixon and his wife, Pat, were both killed while in bed. Their throats were slit. Word had it that the assassination was carried out by Communist cells within the United States. Joseph McCarthy began a special investigation. It was an era of great paranoia. I did not approve of what Santa and Randy did.

THE INQUIRY

I was paid a visit by three Secret Service agents in black suits, black ties, wearing fedoras. They asked me to come with them. I knew I didn't have a choice. I didn't resist. They took me to a warehouse in the middle of nowhere and sat me in a room with mirrors all around. There were five agents talking to me and I knew there were other people behind the mirrors. They said they knew all about my connection with Santa Claus and the assassination of Hitler. "We've always known," they said.

I shrugged.

They asked: "What do you know about the murder of Richard M. Nixon?"

I replied: "All I know is what I read in the papers."

"Don't believe everything you read in the papers, midget."

"I'm a dwarf."

"Same difference."

"I want a lawyer."

"Why?"

"It's my right.

"You have no rights here."

"Excuse me, didn't we get rid of the Nazis? Isn't this America?"

"Talk to us."

"I am talking."

"We know who did it."

"Did what?"

"Who killed the V.P.?"

"Who?"

"You tell us."

"I don't know."

"We believe you do."

"Don't always trust your beliefs, son."

"You getting funny, midget?"

"That's *dwarf.*"

"You want me to toss you?"

"How far?" I asked.

"He's a funny one."

"I try my best," I said.

They said: "We have been tracking Santa. We know he came to see you not too long ago."

"So what?"

"We think he killed Nixon."

I laughed.

"What's so funny, short guy?"

"That," I said, "is absurd."

"On the contrary," they said, "we believe he was behind it."

I asked: "How could you possibly track Santa? He's a spirit and not in our time."

All the Secret Service agents smiled and one said: "We have our ways."

"I know nothing," I said.

"We think you know a lot."

"I don't know doodly-squat," I said.

It went on and on like that for hours, and then they gave up and let me go.

THE GHOST OF NIXON

All I wanted to do was sleep after they took me home. I'm sure my house was bugged. I didn't care. I just wanted to close my eyes and forget everything. But the dead wouldn't allow that. Richard Nixon came to see me. He was wearing a suit and appeared quite grim and angry.

—*Tell them,* said Nixon, *tell them who murdered me.*

"Go away."

—*Tell them the truth!*

"I don't know anything!"

—*You know enough, you three foot and a half motherfucker!* screamed the ghost of Nixon. —*You know enough to put that red-suited fucker in jail and that red-nosed monster in a meat grinder!*

"They said you are the monster."

—*I am no monster, and I am no crook!*

"Yeah, yeah, yeah," said I, "now please go away please so I can get some shuteye, bub."

—*Never,* said Nixon. —*Never until you tell them what you know!*

"I know nothing."

—*I was assassinated!*

It was then that my parents, Nadia, Gabriel, and many whom I had known during the resistance appeared and restrained Nixon from harassing me any further. They dragged him through a door of light, and they told me to rest, they told me to sleep.

And I did.

APPENDIX A

My Letter

Dear Santa Claus,

I hope you will get this, but I know (deep down) you will never get this. I just wanted to say I have never given you and Randy away. I have been terrorized, harangued, followed, watched and investi-gated by many branches of the U.S. government, but there's noth-ing they can do to me that will make me talk. They have hinted at going after my children and grandchildren but I know "they know" that would be a terrible mistake. They are, proverbially speaking, grasping at straws. But I am writing to say that while I do not agree with what you and Randy did, because I realize you had your reasons, was it really the best thing to do? So JFK won the election, but even he was shot and killed, and now we are at our "cold war" with Russia and we live in a land of paranoia and fear where no one trusts their brother or neighbor, and people turn other people in all the time as "enemies of the state" and innocent lives are ruined. Perhaps you should have let things run their course. Had you not killed Nixon, would Kennedy not have nuked Cuba? Think of all the lives there. And now Lyndon Johnson is in power and he has nuked Vietnam and Laos and Cambodia. Where does the senseless killing end? Didn't we see enough? Or is that our nature, to forever murder each other with new weapons of mass destruction? Or are the major wars of history, whatever history it is, inevitable no matter what? I know Hitler had to die, and perhaps Nixon too. But am I happy about it? No. I am haunted every day.

MICHAEL HEMMINGSON

But I will die soon, and then I will have to be ghost, at which point I am sure I will have to stand a celestial trial for all my worldly crimes. I will stand tall, I'm sure. I regret nothing.

Your friend forever,

William Stonecutter

APPENDIX B

My Memory

Berlin—Santa held Hitler down.

Hitler was very confused.

Randy had a knife in his mouth—a long and sharp blade.

"William," Santa said, "do it!"

"Why?" said Hitler. "Why?"

"Must you ask," I said.

"Why?" said Hitler.

"Like the little man said," said Santa, "why ask why?"

"What did I do?!" said Hitler.

I laughed. Santa laughed. Randy shook his head.

The only light in Hitler's bedroom was the glow of the reindeer's nose.

Eva Marie Braun was not there with her husband, and she was lucky for that.

"William," said Santa, "do it now!"

I took the knife from Randy's mouth.

"Make it quick," said the reindeer.

"Do it now," said Santa, "so we can get the hell out of here."

I slit Hitler's throat, I slit it open with two swipes, I opened up his flesh, and my moves were effective.

Blood flew out of the man in every direction like…like blood flowing out in every direction.

Santa released his grip, and let the Nazi leader slide down to the floor to bleed and die.

The three of us stood there until we knew life had left him.

—*Why?* asked the ghost of Hitler, jumping out of his body.

But his ghost was carried away by tall illuminating beings with white robes and golden hair that I had never seen before; and I never saw or spoke to Hitler again.

"It's done," Santa said.

"Let's go get drunk now," Randy the Red-Nosed Reindeer said.

I said, "Let's."

And we did.

And that's that.

www.ingramcontent.com/pod-product-compliance
Lightning Source LLC
Chambersburg PA
CBHW020657180626
46816CB00003B/1327